WARNING

This book contains sexually explicit scenes and adult language. It may be considered offensive to some readers. This book is for sale to adults ONLY.

* * * * * * * * * * * * * * * *

Please store your files wisely where they cannot be accessed by underage readers.

ISBN-13: 978-1988083087
ISBN-10: 1988083087

Other Books by Carla Coxwell:

<u>Torrid Exposure New Adult Romance Series</u>

April is finished with school and ready to build a career. Coming from a well-to-do family, she has decided to reboot her life completely. With family scars too deep to mend, April craves a fresh start. But the past is harder to shake than April ever would have imagined. At the center of it all is Bennett, an old family friend who is the heir to a billionaire media mogul company. Bennett and April haven't been able to stand each other since they were kids. But as the world shifts, the two of them discover the past might be the key to their future.

<u>Devil's Advocate BBW MC New Adult Romance Series</u>

When Kristie comes home from college, the last thing she is expecting is her world to be turned upside down by the appearance of her step-brother, Gray. Gray is rash, impulsive and breaks the law. Kristie's mom asks if she can try to befriend Gray, in hopes to get him on the straight and narrow. The plan backfires, however, as Kristie finds herself falling for Gray. Is it possible he feels the same way? The connection between them threatens to tear down everything Kristie has ever held dear.

<u>Fifty Recipes For Disaster New Adult Romance Series</u>

Trying to win a competition for best chef is cut-throat business. Kiara Sands has just won the opportunity of a lifetime. When she arrives at Fission, she has no idea just how much her life is going to change. She's immediately introduced to Jenny Foster and Robbs Martin, her competitors in the cut throat competition. The only thing Kiara finds more distracting than Robbs' hateful attitude is the handsome executive chef, Paul Weston. It doesn't help matters that Paul is quite taken by Kiara, and showers her with more attention than he gives her competitors.

<u>Star Bright New Adult Romance Series</u>

Torn between her feelings for her agent, Jon, and Rich, a charming bad boy who has ties in the movie industry, Jenny finds herself working through her own past to try to get a grip on her present. As she struggles to learn the lesson that in Hollywood not everyone is what they appear to be, Jenny tries to become a person that she can be proud of. Will she be able to find love and success in Hollywood? Or will she be dragged down by her past forever?

Get the latest update on new releases from the author at:

https://www.carlacoxwell.com/newsletter

This book is Part Three of the "<u>Obsessed Bounty Hunter Romance Series</u>"

1 - Secrets Revealed

Jacqui Schneider couldn't help it. Every time the memories of her family's brutal murder haunted her, she had to escape. The only thing that could replace her sorrow was sex... and lots of it. And so Jacqui developed a pattern of self-destruction by sleeping with random men that she picked up at a local hotel bar. One day, Uncle Max, an old family friend, appeared. He revealed a secret about her father that would change her life forever.

2 - Heart Surrendered

Jaqui thought the training was tough. But keeping her mind concentrated on her task was even tougher after meeting her new trainer. Adam had a rugged handsome face and ripped abs. She hated that Adam was so demanding. Jacqui's boxing technique was never up to his standards. How can she hate someone so much and yet feel such strong attraction? Was he flirting with her while trying to show her the correct stance? If so, the game of seduction was on.

3 - Rapid Pulse Bounty

With her new skills fully developed, Jacqui was a confident bounty hunter with a few successful captures under her belt. Things were looking up for her. The only thing missing in her life right now was Adam. She hadn't seen him since before her first successful mission. He had left before she could show off her triumph. Jacqui admitted to herself that she was in love with a man who belonged to someone else.

Obsessed Bounty Hunter Romance Series

Rapid Pulse Bounty

Book Three

By Carla Coxwell

Copyright Revelry Publishing 2015

Table of Contents

Chapter One

JACQUI SCHNEIDER gazed at her naked reflection in the mirror and liked what she saw. She had always been curvaceous since her breasts started to form when she was sixteen years old. She got that from her mom. But unlike her mom, whose modest virtues bordered on obsessive, Jacqui loved to flaunt her sexiness even as a teenage girl.

But since hooking up with Uncle Max at *The Agency*, the daily rigors of the exercise routines the old man made her go through every day certainly managed to give her muscles the tone that wasn't there before. Her shoulders seemed broader, giving the illusion of a smaller waistline that curved down to her hips. Her round ass was perky as she gave it a playful smack. Her toned arms and legs gave her body the overall impression of a well-oiled machine. Sweating profusely after a five mile run, her sunburned milky-white skin had a pinkish tinge.

After her first assignment went better than expected, Jacqui gained a certain confidence that she never felt before. The next three captures were just as successful. Everything was going well for her. The changes she saw in her body were merely icing on the cake. Every successful capture meant more money in her pocket. It would never replace the loneliness she felt in being alone without mom, dad, and Danny, but it was a good start. Jacqui mulled over in her mind how to spend some of it. Travel, perhaps? But that decision was a long way off from today.

The thought that she would never have to worry about money in the future gave her a sense of security she lost when her whole family was murdered. The easy fifty thousand dollars that she earned from four bounty works had been deposited in the bank, together with the money her dad left her.

"Not bad…" Jacqui whispered in approval over her finances as well as the reflection staring back at her. Picking up the heap of dirty clothes from the floor and grabbing a robe along the way, Jacqui entered the bathroom of her new apartment. Uncle Max helped her settle into her new digs. He insisted that Jacqui come down to the headquarters every day and keep up with her training. So Jacqui opted for a modest townhouse in a quiet neighborhood five miles away. It was a two bedroom affair, furnished, thus sparing her the tedious task of shopping for her own furniture. The living room and kitchen were roomy enough to keep her comfortable during the times she was home.

The only indulgence she added was a shower stall with overhead rainfall shower, a handheld shower hose and 6 body jets. Plus the whirlpool bathtub that Uncle Max declared was a waste of good money. Jacqui insisted that taking long showers was an indulgence and won the argument. This was where she retreated after grueling days of tracking her prey, oftentimes foregoing the luxury of a plain shower when she was on the road.

Jacqui adjusted the knobs of the whirlpool and watched as the water churned gently against the edges of the tub. She lit a few incense candles and poured lavender bath oil into the water.

She stepped gingerly into the warm water and slithered her whole body against the tub. She closed her eyes and sighed in bliss, basking in the floating sensation, making her feel weightless. She allowed her mind to roam, setting free all thoughts and stresses that accompanied her job. But it was also during times like these that thoughts she had buried deep in the recesses of her psyche often crept out of their screened-off area where she had buried them.

Like Adam…

She hadn't seen or heard from him since that day she made her first successful bounty. The revelry that accompanied her return wasn't enough to cover up the intense disappointment she felt when she was told he left with Sarah. She cried herself to sleep that night, after admitting to herself the true status of her heart. She had fallen in love with him… fallen in love with a man who belonged to someone else.

Often, she cursed the day they met. Cursed the seduction he laid out for her. She blamed herself for trying to defeat him in his own game which ended with them having sex on the boxing ring floor. His intoxicating scent, the smell of his breath, the steely feel of his arms around her waist, the powerful thrusts as he entered her astride on his hips.

Jacqui crossed her arms around herself longing for Adam's lean arms. Then she uncrossed them to caress the skin of her throat, shoulders, and belly. They felt velvety and smooth to the touch. Unwittingly, her hands moved to her breasts as she lay immersed in the warm frothy water. She cupped both and let the thumbs and forefingers of each hand play with her nipples. She felt them harden under her ministrations as twinges of sexual pleasure traveled down her groin.

Jacqui enjoyed the feeling of her fingers as they slowly moved down to her cunt. Using two fingers, she opened the lips of her labia and let her clit pop out. The whirlpool massaged her clit gently. It felt really good. She rubbed her exposed nub and added pressure with her finger. Her back arched as a spike of pleasure signaled her arousal. Jacqui raised herself up from the tub and sat down against the rim. She opened her legs wide as she straddled two sides of the tub. She knew what she wanted, what she needed badly.

She picked up a bottle of lube and applied some on her fingers. Then she positioned her fingers against her vagina and rubbed her clit gently. The heat started to build within her open legs. As the heat mounted inside her, Jacqui added more and more pressure on her clit until it felt on fire. She knew her orgasm was near. She imagined Adam's lips as they flicked repeatedly on her clit when he had her prone on the mat. As the intense heat flaring between her legs became too much to bear, she gave in to a powerful orgasm, uttering Adam's name over and over again.

<<◇>>

An hour and fifteen minutes later, Jacqui entered the gate of *The Agency* complex. She wanted to practice on the punching bags. Jerking off today left her feeling lethargic. Instead of diminishing the longing for Adam which she had buried deep inside, it left her with the feeling of wanting more.

"A few rounds on the mat may do me some good," Jacqui thought to herself. She dressed up in black compression short shorts which only served to draw attention to her booty. A white razor back t-shirt that ended just above her navel completed her training outfit. Uncle Max saw her arrive in her car and called out to her.

"I have something for you…come inside, Jac," Uncle Max said leaving the door open. He handed her a parcel wrapped in brown paper and tied with a twine. Jacqui eagerly tore open the package and squealed in joy. Inside was a pink and gray Walter PPK handgun. It was slim and at 6 inches long, fitted perfectly in the palm of her hand.

"Oh, Uncle Max, thank you…it's…it's perfect," Jacqui declared as she gave the old man a hug. "Eli and I were discussing the best weapon for you and we both agreed this is it," Uncle Max said, obviously happy they made the right choice for her.

And then as an afterthought, the old man declared, "You're a good shot Jac, just like your dad. Keep up your practice with Eli. Learn the characteristics of your gun until it becomes an extension of your hand." "Yes… yes… I will…" an elated Jacqui replied before dropping the gun into her purse. "Ready to kick some ass?" Uncle Max asked, eying her tight shorts and even tighter tees. "Nah…just the punch bags for now…" Jacqui replied with a wink. "Well…I'm glad coz I don't think anyone will win against you in that outfit…" Uncle Max retorted with laughter in his voice.

The gym was quiet. Nobody was around today using the ring or flexing muscles on the punch bag. This suited Jacqui just fine. She was in no mood for company. She started with five hundred jump ropes to break out a sweat before donning the gloves and approaching the bag hanging from the ceiling. With light punches, she danced around the bag to improve her footwork. Then she moved on to combination punches. She focused her concentration on her fists just like Adam taught her.

"It's not about strength, but how you use your fists to deploy the power of your punch… " she remembered him saying. With every punch the hapless bag took, Jacqui felt she was pounding her unrequited feelings back into the compartment inside her heart where she had reserved a special lock and key for it. She only slowed down when the darkened hall was suddenly illuminated by sunbeams streaming from the doorway as someone entered the room.

Curious to see who the newcomer was, Jacqui stopped momentarily to greet the new arrival. The sun was shining directly into the open doorway. The silhouette was shrouded in the glow coming from the sun overhead. It took Jacqui's eyes a few seconds to adjust from the darkened interiors as she eyed the

shimmering form bathed in sunshine. When the
newcomer closed the door behind, Jacqui gave a gasp
of surprise.

The figure was shirtless, as usual. The denim jeans
hung carelessly below the hips, emphasizing the flat
stomach and the six pack abs. The hair hanging just
above the shoulders still needed a haircut. It had a
reddish tint over the burnished brown color that it used
to be. The smile still held the same combination of a
mock and a naughty grin.

The figure was unmistakable. It was Adam.

Chapter Two

Jacqui was in a state of shock. She didn't know if the figure leisurely walking toward her was a figment of her imagination… a deception her mind was playing on her pining heart.

"Hello Jacqui," Adam greeted her with a nonchalant smile on his face. "Hi…Adam," Jacqui squeaked, her throat barely able to make the words come out. And then she realized she needed to say something more than just a mundane hi.

"Err… you're here… it's nice to see you back… when did you get ba… ?" she managed to stammer words that fell over each other. Fuck, nice didn't even come close. She was ecstatic, euphoric, overjoyed. Now if she could only unfreeze her brain so she didn't sound catatonic. Jacqui reached out her hand to shake his in greeting just as Adam moved forward and clasped her in an embrace.

Another awkward moment… welcome, but totally unexpected. Jacqui hoped he wouldn't notice how wildly her heart was fluttering inside her chest as her feelings struggled to surface from their stronghold.

"Last night…" Adam answered before releasing her from his arms. "Last night?" Jacqui mimicked, feeling

like a parrot. "Oh… you arrived last night." "Yah…
Uncle Max has been updating me with things around
here. Heard you're doing great," Adam replied with a
sideways glance, uncertainty written on his face. What
was wrong with her?

"Well, yah… err… thanks…" Jacqui once again
stumbled through her vocabulary which seemed to have
shrunk to four- or five-letter words. Why did he have
such an effect on her composure? Surely he had no idea
about her feelings for him. "Uncle Max said I'd find
you here… you look great, Jacqui," Adam said eyeing
her and obviously liking what he saw.

Jacqui flushed under his intense gaze and felt naked
once again. "Feel like doing a round with me?" Adam
teased her. "No… no, thanks, I was just cooling down
when you came," Jacqui replied although she felt a stab
of disappointment. What she really wanted to say was,
Hell yeah… bring it on…

Adam laughed at her discomfiture, reading her
thoughts. He took a seat in the exact spot on the boxing
ring where he fucked her. Jacqui knew that he did it on
purpose. As if to remind her of what took place on that
mat. "So…fill me in… what happened when you were
out there…?" Adam tapped the empty space beside
him, inviting her to sit.

Gingerly, as if walking on eggshells, Jacqui
positioned herself beside him. She thought she wouldn't
have the words to convey to him everything she felt
when she was out there all alone. But Adam's
encouraging demeanor made it easy. She told him about

the long hours of sitting and waiting for her prey to make their appearance, the dismay she felt when she lost track of their whereabouts, the sudden adrenaline rush when she recovered their tracks, her anxiety when she had them within her sight just before she made a call to confirm their location, and the euphoria that accompanied her after each successful bounty.

"Oh, Adam, it's the best feeling in the world…" she gushed. "Better than an orgasm?" Adam asked impishly. Jacqui nudged him playfully with her shoulder. She can be cool with him. After all, she did decide to start a friendship with the rascal. "Oh… I almost forgot… Uncle Max wants to see you in his office," Adam said, jumping from the edge of the boxing ring, holding out his hand to help her down.

Jacqui reached out to accept his assistance, a thrilling buzz running through her palm, up her elbow, through her shoulders and straight into her heart with the sudden contact. She was alarmingly aware that he didn't let go of his grip as they made their way towards the door and out into the open to see the old man.

Uncle Max was sitting behind his table, a stack of documents spread out before him.
"Ahh…good…you're both here," he greeted them, indicating the two chairs in front for them to sit on. "Meet Malcolm Leech, 33 years old, originally from Havana, but managed to acquire U.S. citizenship, second in command to an arms dealer who is so elusive, the DEA thinks it's almost impossible to catch him.

Leech has a bounty on his head for $750,000 and his boss at a million dollars, caught alive. They supply ammo for the different street gangs - Hispanics, Latinos, Mexicans, and Blacks. Mostly from the Chicago area. No discrimination. You show money, they deliver," the old man informed them.

"Why has the DEA been unsuccessful if they sell to anyone…?" Adam asked. "They have powerful connections… their reach is so high they seem to be always a step ahead of the DEA, who suspects a mole in their department. The DEA realized they couldn't do anything using their own agents so they deployed someone else months ago to do the sting. Word on the street now is Leech has just received fresh delivery, more than they can handle. His boss does not feel it is in safe hands. With too much ammo lying around, it's bound to attract the attention of the authorities. He is pressuring Leech to find buyers, pronto. That's all we know."

"So the DEA approached you, asking help in tracking the whereabouts of this Leech…" Jacqui concluded. But Uncle Max cut in before she could finish her sentence and said, "Not just track the guy, but pose as interested buyers, and hopefully, set up a meeting with the brains behind the organization."

"Do we have a photo of him?" Jacqui asked, curious to see the face of the man behind it all. "Unfortunately, this is all we have," Uncle Max said, handing them a 4x6 glossy. Adam and Jacqui peered at the photograph. It was a grainy shot taken with a telephoto lens from a distance. The man wore a grey overcoat with a hat pulled low over his head. The shot showed part of his forehead, a nose, and a sharp chin, as he was about to board a plane. For some inexplicable reason, Jacqui felt agitated. It could have been a picture of anyone. But the outline of the man was strangely familiar. She shrugged it off, thinking it was just her imagination playing tricks on her.

"That photo was taken less than six months ago and the DEA has no idea where he is hiding," Uncle Max said. Adam and Jacqui handed the pictures back to the old man. He was suddenly very serious. "I want both of you to go in and pose as buyers. As I mentioned, the DEA is afraid there is a mole buried deep within their department. Both of you fit the profile of someone this Leech could trust," Uncle Max pointed out to Adam and Jacqui.

Adam and Jacqui looked at each other. There was a glint of excitement in Adam's eyes. Jacqui was excited about this development. Uncle Max must believe in her, enough to trust her with an assignment this big. That, and the fact that she will be working with Adam made the whole experience seem surreal. She forgot the initial foreboding she felt when she saw the grainy picture of the man behind the organization.

The very next day, both boarded a domestic flight to Chicago. The two-hour and thirty-minute flight was spent going through the minute details of their M.O. and surfing through the internet with a notebook.

Johnny 'The Eye' Rodriguez's expertise with equipment and technology had allowed him to hack through the internet and bombard it with articles about their 'escapades'. There were pictures of both Adam and Jacqui skiing on the slopes of Aspen, running with the bulls in Spain, Adam racing at The Formula One, Jacqui sunbathing in Hawaii, all very realistic, and every single one a complete hoax.

Jacqui giggled at a copy of her photo-shopped bikini clad body, dancing with a glass of wine in her hand. Jacqui had two left feet and never danced in her entire life. "That looks so much like you," whispered Jacqui, pointing to a photo of Adam wearing a black racer jacket and preppy Persols. "That's because it's really me… " he whispered back with a hint of laughter in his voice.

"You used to race?" Jacqui inquired, with amazement in her voice. "Uh-huh… still do…"Adam replied with a nod of his head. "Gosh… there's so much I don't know about you…" Jacqui replied, suddenly feeling aghast about her curiosity.

"What do you wanna know…?" Adam asked casually. "Well for starters, where's Sarah, your girlfriend? I haven't seen her since you got back," Jacqui asked quickly before she could change her mind. Adam let loose a guffaw which attracted the attention of some passengers nearby. Then he stood up and pretended to point at her while drawing circles beside his brain, miming she was crazy.

"Sit down," an embarrassed Jacqui hissed. "For starters, Ms. Busybody…Sarah is not my girlfriend, she's my stepsister. Whoever told you she was, should have their head examined," Adam stated, with a puzzled look on his face.

"Well… err… no one said, really. I just assumed when I caught you two together, locked in an embrace outside the building," Jacqui explained, a wild blush turning her face red. "You were snooping on us?" Adam teased her mercilessly. "No… no… of course not. It was an accident. I didn't know you guys were there until I almost ran into you," Jacqui denied vehemently.

Adam leaned back in his seat and said, "My sister has some serious issues. That night you saw us… she came to me and told me she was above her head in gambling debts with some syndicate. It was her boyfriend who got her hooked. I tracked those bastards down, paid off her debts, but not before breaking some bones. I warned them and her boyfriend that if they ever come near her again, I would kill them. Sarah is now in a facility where I hope she gets her head back on straight."

Jacqui was speechless. She was totally embarrassed by her wrong assumption. But at the same time, her heart was soaring and her brain wanted to explode. Sarah was his stepsister… not his girlfriend. Best news ever. "Wait a minute…is that why you have been acting so aloof, so cold to me…because you thought I had a girlfriend? You were jealous," Adam said with certainty.

Jacqui leaned back with a Mona Lisa smile on her face and closed her eyes, pretending to sleep. In a girl's psyche, when cornered with the truth, the best defense is silence.

Chapter Three

When the plane touched down in Chicago, a limo waiting for them by the curb brought them straight to The Trump Hotel along Michigan Avenue. They were shown adjoining suites that overlooked the Chicago River. It took Jacqui's breath away. Uncle Max pulled out all the stops to create the suitable scenario. After all, two rich kids wouldn't check into a dump.

They had no idea how long it would be before they would hear from the undercover agent who was facilitating the meeting with Leech. This was like a grand vacation for Jacqui, although she didn't want to lose sight of the dangers surrounding the sting. Jacqui ran to her side of the double doors of the adjoining suite and opened Adam's door without even bothering to knock.

A naked Adam greeted her eyes. Obviously, the guy wanted to take a quick shower because he had a towel in his hand. All his discarded clothes were in a pile on the floor. "Oh… oh… oh… I'm so sorry… I should have knocked first…" Jacqui said, her face in flames.

She flew back to her side of the room and shut the door quickly, after which she sagged weakly onto the floor. She could swear she heard Adam's laughter from behind the closed door. "Stupid… stupid… stupid…"

she castigated herself, slapping her forehead with her palm.

Picking up the remnants of her lost dignity, she decided she might as well take a shower too. She was feeling sticky after the long flight. Chicago was muggy this time of year.

Jacqui whistled in awe as she opened the door leading to the bathroom. The bathroom occupied half the size of the entire suite. A walk-in closet was on one side with floor to ceiling cabinets in rosewood. The center of the room was occupied by a Jacuzzi with pink marble tiles wrapped around it. The floor tiles, also of pink marble, led all the way to the shower stall in the corner enclosed in Plexiglas. A Tallboy unit held the washbasin just beside the bathroom stall. Gold and crystal accents dominated the room and reflected the lights coming from lamps mounted on the walls.

Jacqui eagerly stripped off all her clothes, forgetting her faux pas with Adam. She entered the stall and lifted her face up the rainfall shower head. The water, which was just the right temperature, felt heavenly as it dripped down her body. The splash coming down from the shower muffled the sound of the shower stall door as it opened. Jacqui hardly noticed that Adam had entered until he whispered in her ear.

"Hope you don't mind if I join you…" Adam said. A startled Jacqui swiveled around. She had no words. Adam lifted her chin up with his finger, their faces inches away from one another. And just before his lips descended down on hers, Jacqui realized it would be futile to resist him. This is what she had been pining the entire time while he was away.

Adam's kiss was deep and probing. He bit gently on her lower lip as his tongue tried to pry them open. Jacqui responded and allowed him access, opening her lips as her tongue met his. Adam reached out behind her to close the shower. His arms then snaked across her back, hands gently exploring the curves leading to her ass. Jacqui was intensely aware of his erection hitting the love spot of her vagina. She reached out her hands to stroke the smooth, hard penis.

Adam grabbed her stroking hand and entwined both arms across his neck before lifting her and carrying her out the bathroom and into the bedroom. He laid her gently across the bed as Jacqui's wet body left an imprint on the satin duvet. Adam stared deeply into her eyes, his prone body atop hers. "Do you want to do this?" he asked her. Jacqui peeled away all reticence and reserve, and answered, "Yes…"

A triumphant smile lit up Adam's eyes before he kissed her again. The kiss was everything Jacqui ever dreamt of. Passionate and romantic, deep and searing, it touched the very recesses of her soul. It was a kiss coming from a soul that was her perfect match... her soul mate.

Adam was a torrid lover. He brought her to heights of passion she did not know existed. He was alternately gentle and savage as he thrust deep into her. Then he would arouse her all over again as he nipped, sucked, and bit her skin. His tongue did not hold restraint as he explored every fold of her pussy, torturing her clit with his unrelenting tongue.

Jacqui thought she had no more to give as her body racked in multiple orgasms. But Adam found reserves that she did not know she had. When she came again for the third time, she felt her body would dissolve from the pleasure. An exhausted Jacqui lay quietly in the nook of Adam's arm. She had never been more thoroughly fucked in all her life. She suddenly felt shy being with him and buried her face into his chest. Adam's arms were like steel bands holding her tightly next to him. His next words established what her heart already knew since the first time they met. "I think I'm in love with you, Jacqui Schneider," Adam said.

Chapter Four

The call from the undercover agent came at 0600 hours the following day. Jacqui was alerted when Adam pulled away from her as he answered the phone. A few seconds later he turned towards her, still nestled within the covers of the bed and whispered in her ear.

"Sorry babe, it's time," Adam said. Months of training had adjusted Jacqui's mind and body to react swiftly. She half-opened her eyes to see his beautiful face inches away from her own. "Hi…" Jacqui whispered dreamily. How can a face rouse desire within her when half of her was still in slumber? Adam gave a naughty grin, reading her thoughts. He stood abruptly and sighed deeply, regretting the lost opportunity to be inside her once again. He headed straight for the bathroom door. Both knew they had a job to do.

Reluctantly, Jacqui hauled her body up, grabbing the duvet to cover her nakedness. She strode to her own bathroom in the adjoining suite. She wanted to take a long shower and if she joined Adam, who knows where things would lead. No. She had to get her head straight. There was danger for both of them up ahead. It was necessary to have a clear head.

She fought the elation that was bubbling in her chest. Adam was in love with her. He said it. Or did she dream it all? Then she must have dreamt about the way he kissed her, and tenderly suckled her breasts, and made love to her over and over again…

"Stop it, Jacqui Schneider…" she objected to her thoughts. A cold shower was exactly what restored her as she dressed quickly. Adam called through the open doorway that he would be meeting her in the lobby in ten minutes.

As she entered the lobby, she espied him over at the reception counter with a suitcase by his side. "Ready?" Adam asked. Jacqui nodded her head in agreement. She sensed that he was tense, probably more aware than she was about the danger that lies ahead. Carrying the suitcase, he led her to a Mercedes Benz SUV parked in the curb of the hotel. He opened the door and strapped her in.

As he took the driver's seat, he looked at her seriously and said, "Just follow my lead, Jac. I'll do all the talking." "What's in the suitcase?" she asked curiously. "Twenty-five million dollars and this car are all courtesy of *The Agency*," Adam answered simply. Adam punched in an address in the GPS system of the car. They drove through the main thoroughfares of Chicago until they reached the Tri-State Tollway, then onto an inn with a park across the road.

"Leave your gun in the compartment," Adam ordered Jacqui. "But…" Jacqui started to argue until she saw Adam's face. Gone was the Adam who held her all through the night. His eyes acquired a shade of blue like the waters of the ocean in its deepest places.

His pupils dilated as he scanned his surroundings. The planes of his face resembled cast metal. A predator, focused, unfeeling, aware of the danger lurking ahead. This was a man who lived for the hunt.

"They will frisk us…" Adam said in a cold voice. Bypassing the reception area, Adam and Jacqui took the stairs to the second floor and knocked on a door at the end of the hallway. The door was opened by a mean-looking Hispanic who eyed them suspiciously. "Leech is expecting us…" Adam said in a steely voice.

The door opened wide as Adam and Jacqui entered a small conference room. The curtains were drawn against the windows. An air-conditioning unit was on full blast while a ceiling fan whirred from above, giving the room its only ventilation.

Malcolm Leech was seated by a table. Prominent among his features were the droopy eyes that stared in a sinister way and a cut on the lip giving him a permanent sneer. A diamond stud gleamed from his ear. Two other men stood on each side. One of them played with a gun in his hand. Adam and Jacqui step into the room and headed for the table. A hand dropped on Adam's shoulder and roughly spun him around.

"Not so fast, Amigo…I need to see you're clean," said man who opened the door. Adam stared him directly in the eyes, indicating his displeasure. After a few seconds, he spread out his arms and legs to allow the search. The man nodded towards the direction of the table to indicate Adam was clean. He reached out to do the same to Jacqui when Adam swiftly grabbed hold of his arm, twisted around and held the man in a headlock. The man squealed in pain.

"You can do a body search on me. But touch my girl and we're both out of here, comprende?" Adam said loudly, looking directly at Leech seated on the table. Leech nodded imperceptibly and Adam let go, pushing the man away from him. Adam picked up the suitcase and ushered Jacqui towards the table. "Leech…" he greeted the man in a sneering voice. "Friend, you have the pleasure of knowing who I am but I know almost nothing about you," Leech said amiably.

"You know enough about me. Otherwise you wouldn't have agreed to meet with us. This is not a social call. I am here for business. Tell me what you've got. I want it all," Adam said in an autocratic voice. Jacqui saw Leech blanch in surprise as Adam's words caught him totally by surprise. "We have single shot rifles, an odd assortment of handguns, AK-47s up to military grade assault rifles," Leech reeled off the entire arsenal in their possession.

"That's fine with me…" Adam answered without batting an eyelash. "Can you make the delivery within two days?" Leech hesitated for the first time… a reaction that didn't go unnoticed by both Adam and Jacqui. "Wait… wait a minute…" Leech faltered. "I need to talk to my partner about this."

"I was told you are the man to talk to. Not some fucking runner for someone else," Adam replied with a note of mockery in his voice. Leech showed his displeasure over the insult and stood up menacingly. But Adam was quick to push his advantage. "Look Leech, I came here prepared to pay…" as he opened the suitcase and displayed the bundles of money within, "…not negotiate. You bring your partner here now, or else we walk," Adam upped the ante.

"That's impossible. He never meets with anyone. I do all the negotiating," Leech blustered as he eyes the layers of cash within the suitcase. "Then this is all a waste of my time," Adam said with irritation. He snapped the suitcase shut and walked to the door with Jacqui quickly behind him. Both were aware this was the biggest bait they could play. Either Leech takes the bait or they leave empty-handed.

"Hold on…" Leech called out just as they reached the door. Adam turned around to face him, and raised his brows in an arrogant manner. Leech pulled out his cell phone and talked in a low voice. It was obvious from his face that whoever was at the other end of the line was not happy about the turn of events. Leech gesticulated wildly with his arms, trying to make a point. Then he listened intently, nodded his head, smiled and snapped the phone shut.

"He will be here in twenty minutes. You owe me, man…I convinced him you're worth it…" Leech bragged. Adam felt Jacqui's sigh of relief. But he admired her composure. Her face never lost the insipid but haughty look she wore since the start. Both approached the table once more. Now that the tension had broken between them, Jacqui noted that Leech was friendlier… salivating over the money he would earn.

Jacqui knew she needed to make her move. Fanning her hands to her face, she addressed Adam, "Honey, this room is too warm. I need a breath of fresh air…" The man who met them at the door instantly tensed and made as if to follow her as she headed for the door.

Adam spoke with a pleasant voice and tapped Leech by the shoulder. "Tell your man to leave my girl alone. I don't trust him. I mean, after all, what can a little lady do except roll in bed with you?" Leech and the rest of men, together with Adam, chuckled over this. Jacqui pretended to be displeased and left the room with a snooty swing of her hair. As soon as she hit the hallway, Jacqui hurried down the stairs and headed straight for the SUV. She retrieved her Walter PPK and strapped it between her thighs. She left her purse lying on the table inside the room with Adam. Her cell phone was inside the purse. She would need that later on to make contact. But not yet… the primary target had still to show up.

Jacqui's heart accelerated with excitement. If all goes well today, she would be earning lots of money from this bounty. She could afford to take a vacation, hopefully with Adam along. They could do Hawaii. Her picture was all over the internet anyway, dancing with a glass of wine in her hand. Jacqui glanced at her watch. Twenty minutes were almost up.

God, I hope they don't frisk me when I come in again, she thought nervously. The gun between her thighs was the only protection she and Adam had. But she need not have worried, as everyone hardly looked up when she entered the room once more. They were all huddled around Adam, who was showing them some high powered gadgets on his tablet.

Jacqui knew that Adam intentionally did this to divert attention. He was establishing a bond with all the men, making them feel he was one of them. Nice move, Jacqui thought.

The door opened and everyone looked up. Standing on the threshold was a man of about 60 years of age. Silver streaks of hair were showing beside the temple over a hat that covered the rest of his head. He had a hooked nose, and a pointed chin. Except for the eyes that glinted, one would think he was somebody's grandfather. Jacqui sensed the evil lurking behind those eyes. Leech and the rest of his men all stand respectfully as the commandant approached. It was apparent from their demeanor that this was someone they all feared. The imperious leader cast Jacqui a glance as he passed, and proceeded to approach Adam, who didn't bother to stand.

That one glance was all it took. Recognition was instant as memories come flooding back to Jacqui. This… this was the man she saw that night her family was murdered. This was the man who mercilessly shot her mom before her dad's eyes. This was the man who brutally wiped out the light from Danny's eyes as her dad screamed in rage and fear... the man who ended her dad's life without hesitation.

Jacqui recoiled in a mixture of rage and fear. Her breath came in short gasps as the whole room turned red before her eyes. It took immense effort to stop her body from shaking. She had a clear sight of the back of the old man's head. She could draw the gun from between her thighs and pull the trigger. She knew she could kill him with a single bullet. That would be her revenge for the death of her entire family.

Yet somehow, as all these thoughts swirled in her mind, Jacqui knew his death by her hand would only avenge her. What of all the other crimes this guy had committed to others? This man had to be caught and made to suffer for all the evil he had done. Besides, she was the only one with a gun. Adam was unarmed. Jacqui was certain that with the first gunshot, Leech and all the others would draw their own weapons and start shooting. How many could she take down before Adam got shot? She had to think about Adam too.

Jacqui made a quick decision. She played the beautiful, but asinine girlfriend in this scenario. So she sauntered toward the table, grabbed hold of her purse and declared petulantly, "This is taking longer than I thought. I have to cancel a previous appointment."

Adam waved her off as if humoring a child and continued to huddle with the rest of the group. He was playing his role to perfection. Jacqui casually got her phone from her purse and pressed a number. The alarm was sent instantly. The GPS system in the car was wired to show their location. All Jacqui and Adam had to do was wait.

Less than five minutes after sending the call, all hell broke loose as the door was smashed open. Breaking glass flew everywhere as men entered through the windows. The room was a chaotic scene as the S.W.A.T. team in full military gear flooded into the room. Red dots from sniper sights spotted the heads of the old leader, Leech, and the three others. It would have been foolish for them to even try and aim their guns as it would mean instant death. They knew it. The leader knew it.

"It's over…" he muttered under his breath, raising his hands in surrender. Suddenly, a familiar figure entered the room and headed straight for Jacqui. "Uncle Max," Jacqui said in surprise. "You're here. It's him, Uncle Max. That's the man who killed my whole family."

Jacqui hated to show any sign of weakness, not with Adam and Uncle Max there. But the extent of her emotions got the better of her and she started to cry. Uncle Max hugged her and softly said, "Yes, I know Jacqui. I couldn't tell you earlier because I was afraid your sentiment would get you. I didn't want you to be reckless and make stupid mistakes in your desire for revenge. I know you well enough to know that as soon as you made the connection, you would do the right thing."

"I made a drastic mistake. I should have made sure I killed everyone in your family that night. Then this could have been avoided," the leader declared so casually, as if they were making small talk around the dinner table. Jacqui stared in shock, unable to believe what she just heard. After everything, he still had the gall to taunt her. All the anger she had managed to control till then came flooding back. Anger turned to rage, and rage into boiling fury. She moved away from Uncle Max and ran toward the leader.

"No… no… Jacqui don't," she heard Adam and Uncle Max shout in unison. But Jacqui was beyond control. The potency of her fury gave her feet wings, dashing towards the leader. She raised her elbow, pulled back her arm, closed her fist, and lunged at the leader with a solid punch in the face. The leader fell to a heap on the floor, senseless. Adam could barely restrain a livid Jacqui, even with his arms wrapped around her.

"My girlfriend is pretty cool. She can kick ass," Adam said for all to hear.

Eighteen months later, a verdict of 'guilty for multiple counts of illicit arms dealing and multiple murder charges' was handed down by the Supreme Court. Jacqui made it her personal mission to attend all the trials. It was with huge relief when she heard the verdict and the sentencing – life imprisonment with no possibility of parole – for the whole syndicate. The rest of the gang, who eluded arrest, vanished into thin air. There was no chance of regaining ground with the arrest of both Leech and the leader of the group.

A day after the sentencing, Jacqui walked slowly to the graves of her mom, dad and Danny. It was a cool day with a gentle breeze. Jacqui laid down the flowers she held in her arms. "I got him, dad. I got him for you, mom and Danny…" she whispered as lonely tears form in her eyes.

A second figure joined her as she stood vigil beside the graves. Adam snaked his arm across her waist and gave her a kiss on the cheek. "Say your final goodbyes, Jacqui. There's a whole new life ahead of you…and if you will allow me, I want to be a part of it," Adam said. Jacqui looked up at him and saw the light in those beautiful blue eyes. Her spirit felt free for the first time in a long while. "Yes…" she answered softly.

It was time to move on.

-The End-

If you enjoyed this title, I would appreciate your leaving a review of the book. Good reviews encourage an author to write as well as help books to sell. Good reviews can be just a few short sentences describing what you liked about the book without having a spoiler. If you could spend 30 seconds writing a review, I would appreciate it: you can review this title right now at your favorite retailer.

Here is a preview of **another story** you may also enjoy:

I STEP into my steam shower, seal the door behind me, and turn on the spray. As the hot water falls over my aching muscles, the enclosed walls trap the relaxing steam in the stall. I reach for one of my fancy new aromatherapy body washes and marvel at the way my life has changed in the last month.

I'd arrived in New York City four and a half weeks ago, shell shocked and numbed by Jenny's revelation: Robbs was the father of her unborn child, not Paul. I tried to tell myself that the news didn't change anything, but deep down I knew the truth. If Jenny had been honest from the beginning, Paul and I would still be together. I've been thinking about that a lot since I arrived in the city, and I still can't decide if that would have been a good thing or a bad thing.

The flight landed at JFK Airport at ten p.m. on a cold March night. Having had to take care of myself since the age of sixteen, I'd never had the money to visit Dallas, much less somewhere as far away as New York City. James O'Toole, my new boss, had arranged for a car to pick me up from the airport and take me to The Plaza, where I'd be staying until I found an apartment. I'd told James that I'd be happy to stay somewhere more affordable, but he'd laughed off the suggestion and insisted that I have the best. That was my first sign that life in New York would be unlike anything I'd ever experienced.

As the Town Car carried me through the city, I became so absorbed in my new hometown that I completely forgot about Paul, Jenny, and all of the drama I'd just left behind. New York had an amazing energy, and I was ready to be a part of it. As we crossed the bridge into Manhattan, I pulled out my cell phone and blocked Paul and Jenny's numbers. I wanted to cut all ties with my old life so I could fully experience my new one. All ties that is, except for Chase.

When I arrived at the hotel that first night, a package was waiting for me at the front desk. I waited until I was alone in my elegant room before opening it. The box contained a subway pass, individual maps of each borough, an electronic planner, and an envelope. I broke the seal and found a letter and a Platinum card. The letter was from James, telling me that he'd be out of town for the next month filming the overseas finale of *Kitchen Wars*.

You've got a lot of work to get done before I get back. I've listed forty of the greatest restaurants in the city in the enclosed planner. I expect you to visit all of them and have critiques ready when I return home. I've also made several appointments for you. They are listed in the planner as well. The real estate agent will show you apartments within the budget I authorized. Use the credit card for your meals and to pay everyone else.

I'd immediately scanned through the planner; not only would I be meeting with the real estate agent, I also had meetings scheduled with a hairstylist, a personal shopper, and my new faculty advisor at The Culinary Institute of New York.

My first week in the city was an absolute nightmare. Between making it to all of my appointments and fitting in one of my assigned restaurants, I barely had time to take a breath. But on my third day, I met with the amazing Myra Owens, who showed me my dream home. It was the third apartment I looked at, and I immediately knew that I had to have it. I now live in a spacious studio; it's modern and elegant, with hardwood floors and quartz countertops. It's only a one bedroom, but it's more than enough space for me. I still haven't recovered from the shock of learning just how much James O'Toole was willing to spend to keep me happy in the city.

I lather the citrusy soap over my body and reach for the shampoo that was custom blended for my hair. Frankie, the stylist James had sent me to, was a genius blend of chemist and artist. He'd given me highlights and lowlights and then whipped up several products for me to take home. When I'd pulled out my Platinum card, he'd shaken his head.

"Mr. O'Toole has already taken care of it," he'd told me.

Each of the personal shoppers I'd met with had said the same thing. When I'd called James and insisted that I couldn't accept any more gifts or favors from him, he'd simply laughed.

"I'm in the limelight," he'd explained. "Photographers follow me everywhere I go. As my apprentice, you'll now be photographed just as much as

I am. I insist that you look your best at all times. Anything less would be contradictory to my brand."

From that point on, I hadn't felt bad about spending his money. I ordered everything I wanted from the restaurants I visited, to the point that I often took half of it home for later. I didn't worry about the price of the clothes I bought on Fifth Avenue, and I added enormous tips to every receipt I signed. After all, generosity had to be good for 'the brand'.

But my four weeks of play time have run out; James flew in last night, and I have to report for my first day on the job in an hour. I turn off the water and step out onto the heated stone floor. I wrap myself in a fluffy towel and head into my closet to decide what to wear. I assume that I'll be spending most of my day in the kitchen, covered in a chef's coat, so I select a pair of lightweight black slacks and a designer white silk T-shirt. I put on a light layer of makeup before sliding into the clothes and blast my hair with a blow dryer. I stop with my hair still a bit damp, gather it in the middle of my head, and weave it into an intricate braid. I twist the braid into a bun, secure it with bobby pins, and pronounce myself ready for the day.

If you enjoyed this sample then look for **Fifty Recipes for Disaster, Book 3.**

Here is a preview of **another story** you may also enjoy:

Torrid Exposure - Book 1

"**I THINK** it looks nice."

"Are you crazy? It isn't even at all."

"Well, you do it then, April."

I sigh and take a step forward, looking at the photo that Emily had hung up in the living room. It looks crooked to me. Okay, maybe just a little off center. I lean forward and nudge it slightly with my finger. It slides just over enough to look perfectly center to me and I look back at her.

Emily is wearing an amused expression on her face. "Oh, yeah, massive difference."

I know she is teasing me. I roll my eyes and look back at the photo. I hear Emily leaving the room to go finish unpacking in her own bedroom. I look around the living room. The big things seemed to be unpacked. I sit down on the couch and sink into it, relaxing my feet for a moment.

Moving felt as if it had taken ages. I am glad to see that the big things are all unpacked. Now I can try to relax for the night. Even though it is hot outside, part of me wants to bundle up underneath a pile of blankets and go to sleep.

But I get up and make myself walk to my own bedroom. *My own bedroom*. It sounds foreign to me. Not that I haven't ever *had* my own bedroom. Of course, I had my own bedroom when I lived at home.

But I shared a dorm room in college so I wasn't exactly dealing with the utmost of privacy.

Now, however, I have a space all to myself. The only other person in this apartment is Emily, my best friend since I was little. Finally, it feels as if life is falling into place.

I sit down on the floor and start going through one of the boxes. I have always been terrible at packing. I usually end up shoving everything in boxes without any sort of organization at all. I never learn, apparently, because this current box has everything from clothes to my laptop. At the bottom, I yank something out. It is a photo album. This is weird… I didn't put this in here.

I flip it open to a random photo and see myself at age six. My skinny arms are wrapped around my sister, who is beaming at the camera. Behind her is a water slide. We must have been at some water park.

I scowl. My sister, Spencer, must have slipped this in the box. It was most likely a last ditch attempt at getting me to reach out to her.

"It isn't going to work," I say out loud and shove the photo album back in the box.

Emily sticks her head in inquiring, "Did you say something?"

"Yeah. Not to you though. Just…" I bite my bottom lip, "… just that Spencer shoved this stupid photo album in one of the boxes. I didn't notice it until now."

Emily is staring at me, clearly trying to figure out what to say next. She, of all people, knows the relationship I have with my family and that it isn't the best. But I don't want to ruin our day of getting our own place with mention of them so I quickly shake my head.

"No, it's cool, really. I'm just going to finish unpacking in here."

"Okay," she replies and turns around to leave before hesitating. "Listen, April. You know if you need to talk about them, you can. You don't have to lock it all up inside."

"I know. Thanks."

Emily nods at me and leaves me alone in my bedroom again. My earlier zest at having my own space is now slightly dulled. I sit on the floor and run my fingers over the cover of the photo album. I don't know when Spencer would have snuck this in. Did she really think this would do anything? Knowing her, she probably thought I would see it and decide to move back home.

Well, she is wrong. I stand up and decide to go through another box. If I find another surprise from her in any of these boxes, I am going to lose it on her. But I then think quickly, maybe that is what she wants me to do.

I decide I'll unpack something I like. The big box holding my photography equipment is stacked up against the wall. I yank it over and sit down on the floor again, opening it up and slowly pulling everything out.

Once I am holding my camera, I feel myself calm down a bit. It is state of the art. All my equipment is expensive – and I had purchased it all by myself. No hand-outs from Mommy and Daddy, no matter what anyone may think. I go through the box and organize everything. I was itching to take photos of my room and I took some spontaneous shots. I want to start a photo album of my life beginning with moving out on my own and continue on as I get my career going.

After I finish taking some photos of my room, I grab clean clothes and head into the bathroom for a quick shower. I can hear Emily talking to someone quietly on her phone in the kitchen. It is probably her boyfriend. Ever since Matt and I broke up, she is worried that if I hear her talking to her boyfriend, I might start crying over my failed relationship.

Maybe I would have a couple of months ago. But I am working every day to get over Matt and everything we went through. I tell myself that what we had was just a college romance. Of course it was going to end after graduation. That was what I told everyone after we broke up. I downplayed how serious we were. I felt like a fool for not seeing it before it happened.

Only Emily knew how hard the break-up hit me. Better not to think about Matt now. I have other things that I need to focus on. Whatever I went through with Matt is in the past now.

I step into the shower to clear my mind. I have things to get arranged. No use in thinking about the past.

If you enjoyed this sample then look for **Torrid Exposure - Book 1**.

Here is a preview of **another story** you may also enjoy:

Romeo Alpha: A BBW Paranormal Shifter Romance - Book 3 by Darla Dunbar

ROMEO FELT groggy as he surveyed his surroundings. The last thing he could remember was saying his vows to the love of his life, Amanda, and then he must have passed out. He was sore all over, and he realized he was tied to a post of some kind. The chill of the wind and the lightness of the atmosphere told him that he was high up in the trees on one of the many mountains near his home, but where was Amanda? Was she all right? Who had tied him up?

He looked down at his shoulder which was aching and saw that a piece of silver was buried deep inside his skin, creating a painful wound. If he could get it out, he could shift if need be. But he would have to get out of the binds that held him first.

Then, squinting in the dark, he saw a figure approaching him. He was about to get his answer. A fire crackled nearby, and he craved the warmth, though he'd prefer the warmth of his bride next to him instead.

"Well, well, look who's awake."

Romeo recognized the voice, and the flames revealed a familiar face. "Remus, what in the hell is going on here? Untie me right now! My mate could be in danger."

"Oh, my friend, I knew this was going to be fun, but you're making it even better for me." Remus' evil grin sent a shiver down Romeo's spine. He pulled something from his jacket, and Romeo froze. "What, you aren't so brave now when you're facing silver bullets? You know, fear isn't going to save you. You see, you've been put entirely in my charge for now. And unless the mate you speak of does as she is told, I get to kill you. As it is, I get to torture you and maim you."

He shot at Romeo; once, twice, three times, burying bullets into his flesh. They hit his arm and his leg in quick succession. Romeo gritted his teeth and tried not to show how much pain he was in. The silver was searing his flesh, ripping through his body. The fire surged through him, and his head felt like it was going to explode. Any hope of shifting and getting out of this mess was gone.

"Damn it, Remus. You used to be one of us. I know you care for Audri and she cares for another, but this is no reason to betray your own kind. What could possibly be in it for you? And where is my mate, my bride? It sounds like you know." Romeo commanded the strength of the alpha to sound as menacing as possible, but he had a feeling Remus was too far gone. This was not the child who had followed his little sister around like a lost puppy dog. This was an evil man looking for blood.

"I'm in it for Audri, of course. She was promised to me if I successfully kept you here until your mate completed the task she was given. You see, I chose to align myself with someone more powerful than either of you could ever hope to be. He will give me everything I wish for. In the end, your stubborn sister will bow at my feet and beg for me to have her."

"Where is Amanda?" Romeo's voice echoed through the dark night, causing Remus to jump a little. Romeo smiled; but Remus shot him with another silver bullet. It hit his knee cap, going through the joint. Romeo screamed out in pain, no longer able to control it.

"Your precious Amanda is probably making her way to Dean right now to give up her powers. It is the only way she is allowed to have you and the other Radiants back, though I may take one of those Radiants for myself."

Romeo was disgusted by the man who was once a friend, the man who might have once had a chance at being his brother-in-law. "I was going to have Amanda, but you have rendered her useless to me, now. The damn mating ritual made it so I can't pleasure her even if I wanted to. Not that any of it matters now. I will have your damn pack anyway once you and your stupid brother are out of the picture."

Romeo couldn't help but chuckle. "I thought part of the plan was to keep me alive. It'll be you who's dead if you go against your orders. Besides, you are no match for me or my wife. She has more power than you could even imagine, and I doubt she'll give it away to that evil man who calls himself her brother. She'll have a plan."

"For your sake, you better hope not, Romeo, because that will certainly mean your death. And I will show no mercy. You will suffer greatly if you die directly at my hand. Now, get some rest. I'm sure you'll need your strength, since you'll be back to procreating with your mate and wife by this time tomorrow night. Though, I'm not sure you'll still want her once she's practically a human. Of course, that's if Dean let's her live. He can be testy, that one. You better pray she keeps her trap shut."

Remus turned to walk away from Romeo, but Romeo pulled a pocket of phlegm from the back of his throat and launched it at Remus. It landed on his cheap Goth boots.

Remus turned around with a snarl. "I said it was time to rest, Romeo, but then again, you never did listen. How does it feel to be pulled off your god-like pedestal and learn you're no better than anyone else?" Remus didn't wait for an answer. He kicked out his boot, the same one Romeo had landed the wad of spit on, and kicked Romeo square in the head. Romeo's world went pitch black as he was knocked into a dreamless sleep.

If you enjoyed this sample then look for **Romeo Alpha: A BBW Paranormal Shifter Romance - Book 3 by Darla Dunbar.**

Other Books by Carla Coxwell

- Torrid Exposure New Adult Romance Series

- Devil's Advocate BBW MC New Adult Romance Series

- Fifty Recipes For Disaster New Adult Romance Series

- Star Bright New Adult Romance Series

Get the latest update on new releases from the author at:

https://www.carlacoxwell.com/newsletter

About the Author - Carla Coxwell

Carla has always been a fan of romance novels. To augment what she made waiting on tables to help her way through college, Carla also did some freelance work in the romance genre.

Now she enjoys living vicariously through her characters in her New Adult Romance books.

Connect with Carla Coxwell

I really appreciate you reading my book! Here are my social media coordinates:

Friend me on Facebook:
https://www.facebook.com/CarlaCoxwell/

Follow me on Twitter: https://twitter.com/carlacoxwell

Check me out on Goodreads:
https://www.goodreads.com/author/show/10691544.Carla_Coxwell

Subscribe to my newsletter:
https://www.carlacoxwell.com/newsletter/

Visit my website: https://www.carlacoxwell.com/